ear Parent:
ur child's love of reading starts here!

'an Read Books have introduced children to the joy of reading
e 1957. Featuring award-winning authors and illustrators and a
ulous cast of beloved characters, I Can Read Books set the
ndard for beginning readers. From books your child reads with
to the first books they read alone, there are I Can Read Books
every stage of reading:

SHARED READING
Basic language, word repetition, and whimsical illustrations,
ideal for sharing with your emergent reader

BEGINNING READING
Short sentences, familiar words, and simple concepts
for children eager to read on their own

READING WITH HELP
Engaging stories, longer sentences, and language play
for developing readers

READING ALONE
Complex plots, challenging vocabulary, and high-interest topics
for the independent reader

ADVANCED READING
Short paragraphs, chapters, and exciting themes
for the perfect bridge to chapter books

ry child learns in a different way and at their own speed. Some
d through each level in order. Others go back and forth between
els and read favorite books again and again. You can help your
ung reader improve and become more confident by encouraging
ir own interests and abilities.

fetime of discovery begins with the magical words, **"I Can Read!"**

For Erica and Laura—
city mouse, country mouse!
—A.S.C.

ISBN-13: 978-0-439-91763-6
ISBN-10: 0-439-91763-8

Text copyright © 2006 by Alyssa Satin Capucilli.
Illustrations copyright © 2006 by Pat Schories. All rights reserved.
Published by Scholastic Inc., 557 Broadway, New York, NY 10012,
by arrangement with HarperCollins Children's Books, a division of
HarperCollins Publishers. I Can Read Book® is a trademark of
HarperCollins Publishers Inc. SCHOLASTIC and associated logos
are trademarks and/or registered trademarks of Scholastic Inc.

36 35 34 33 32 31   13 14 15 16/0

Printed in the U.S.A.   40

First Scholastic printing, January 2007

MY FIRST

I Can Read Book®

Biscuit
Visits
the
Big City

story by ALYSSA SATIN CAPUCILLI
pictures by PAT SCHORIES

SCHOLASTIC INC.

New York   Toronto   London   Auckland   Sydney
Mexico City   New Delhi   Hong Kong   Buenos Aires

Here we are, Biscuit.

Woof, woof!

We're in the big city.

We're going to visit
our friend Jack.

Woof, woof!

Coo, coo!

Stay with me, Biscuit.

It's very busy in the big city!

Woof, woof!

There are lots of tall buildings
in the big city, Biscuit.
Woof, woof!

There are lots of people, too.

Woof, woof!

Funny puppy!
You want to say hello
to everyone.

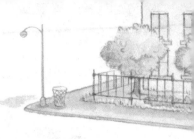

Stay with me, Biscuit.

It's very busy here!

Woof, woof!

Beep! Beep!

Woof!

It's only a big bus, Biscuit.

Woof, woof!

You found the fountain,

Biscuit.

There's so much to see
in the big city,
isn't there, Biscuit?

Woof!

Coo, coo!

Woof, woof!
Coo, coo!

Woof, woof! Woof, woof!
Oh no, Biscuit! Come back!

Biscuit, where are you going?

Woof!

Silly puppy! Here you are.

This is a big, busy city, Biscuit

But you found our friend Jack

and some new friends, too!

Coo, coo!

Woof!